BOB
SHEA

PLANS

LANE SMITH

HYPERION BOOKS FOR CHILDREN NEW YORK

SOON...

the entire world will know of my big plans.

I WILL NOT ROLL MY EYES. I WILL N
I WILL NOT SCHEME IN CLASS. I WILL
WHAT I SAY DOES NOT GO. I AM NOT T
I AM NOT THE BOSS OF THE CLASS. I A
I WILL NOT LAUGH WHEN OTHERS SPEAK.
IT'S NICE TO BE IMPORTANT, BUT IT'S MOR
IMPORTANT TO BE NICE.
I WILL NOT PROVE THE TEACHER WRONG

Plans so big I'll need Dad's
shiniest tie and fanciest shoes.

Then
I'll
climb
atop the
highest
hill in
town and
shout...

"I GOT BIG

BIG

On the way down, I'll meet a mynah bird.

"HEY BIRD, have you heard? I got me some big plans! BIG PLANS, I say.

"What's it gonna be, bird? In or out?"

"I'm in!" says the mynah bird.

"Okay, then! Onward, bird!"

There—there! A city as big as my plans!

"C'MON BIRD, time to talk turkey!
Get down to business!
Go straight to the top!"

"I'm in!" says the mynah bird.

"Listen up, BIG SHOTS, BIGWIGS, What am I dressed for?" I'll ask.

"Success!" they'll yell.

"And what do clothes make?" I'll ask.

"The man!" they'll answer.

Then it should come as no surprise when I say,

"I GOT BIG PLANS! BIG PLANS, I SAY!"

"I'm in!" says the mynah bird.

"YOU! Take a memo! YOU! Hold my calls! YOU! Ready my helicopter!"

"He's got big plans!
Big plans, he says!"
they'll cheer as we take off.

We won't hear them because helicopters are very loud.

"HEY BIRD!
Isn't that the local sports team
losing to the out-of-towners?

XL - 5

"This is not in the plans!" I'll say.
"BIG PLANS, I say!
Let's land this bird, bird."

With seconds left to play, we land, join the team, teach the bird football, and grab a hot dog. Then that mynah bird throws a perfect game-winning pass, which I catch perfectly. The frenzied fans whisk us from the field, shouting,

"He's got big plans!

BIG PLANS, HE SAYS!"

"I'm in!" says the mynah bird.

"WE DECLARE MAYOR!

"What about the old mayor?"

"YOU THE NEW"

declares the crowd.

I'll ask.

"I'm not the one with the big plans!"

he'll say.

If my shirt had sleeves, I'd roll them up.

"YOU! Dig a hole!"

"YOU! Build a school!"

"What's under that skunk?

"A quarter? Why, this skunk is lucky! Hey mynah bird, meet my new stinky lucky hat! Stinky luck, I say!"

"I'm in!" says the mynah bird.

"Now, where was I? WHERE WAS I?"

"OH YES, BIG PLANS!

BIG PLANS, I SAY!

"YOU! Paint the town red!

PAINT IT RED, I SAY!"

This is the part where my cell phone will ring.

"*Brinnnng!*" says the cell phone. "**Hello! Hello!**" I'll say.

"Hi! I'm the president. I heard you got some big plans. How would you like to be assistant president?" he'll say.

"WHAT? Maybe you didn't hear exactly how big my plans are? Big enough to be PRESIDENT president!" I'll say.

"But that's my job!" he'll say.

"Look, are you a naysayer?" I'll say.

"Do you say 'NAY'? I say."

"Uh...no?" he'll say.

"Then it's settled," I'll say.

"You're third in charge, reporting directly to the mynah bird!"

I'd slam the phone down dramatically, but it's a cell phone.

As *president* president, I'll get to be on TV.

"Listen up, states! I got big plans! BIG PLANS, I SAY!"

"PENNSYLVANIA! Build a rocket ship!"

"IDAHO! Make some space suits using the latest potato technology!"

"MISSOURI! Cheer up! You're bringing me down."

"The rest of you, mill about! MILL ABOUT, I say!"

When my rocket is ready and Missouri is happy, bird, hat, and I will blast off into uncertainty!

Or to the moon, whichever.

Once we land, it's straight to work.

"Move that rock, shine this one!
Shift that one left! OTHER LEFT, I say!
Hurry, hurry! Air is low! LOW, I say!
To the ship!
TO THE SHIP, I say!"

As soon as we're safely on the
ship, I will summon my remaining
strength to tell that hat and bird,

"I got big plans,

BIG PLANS, I say."

"I'm innnn,"
the exhausted bird will say.

"Stay with me, bird!" I'll say.
As we race back to Earth,
we will turn to the moon.
There, in the night
sky for all to see,
it will say . . .

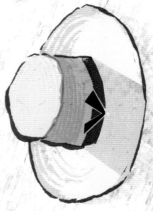

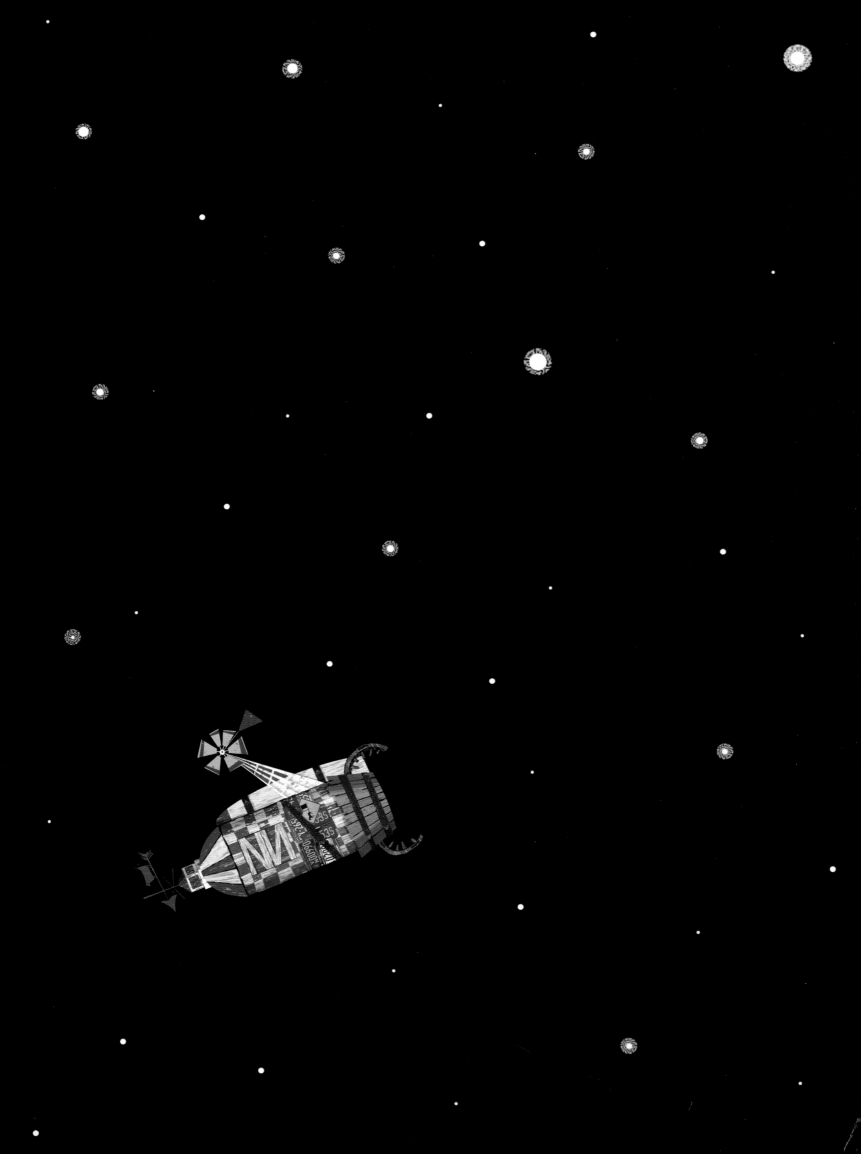

And then the entire world will know of my big plans.

Designed by
Molly Leach